Mel Bay Presents
CHROMATI HARMONICA SOLOS
By Phil Duncan

GW00363935

CD CONTENTS

1	Air On The G String (Orchestra Suite No.3), J.S. Bach [3:36]
2	Sarabande, G.F. Handel [0:51]
3	Andante Cantabile (Symphony No.5), P. Tschaikovsky [2:59]
4	Ave Maria. Franz Schubert [4:04]
5	Brahms' Lullaby, J. Brahms [0:44]
6	Claire De Lune, C. Debussy [2:01]
7	Dreaming (Reverie), C. Debussy [2:09]
8	Drigo's Serenade, R. Drigo [1:09]
9	Emperor Waltz, J. Strauss [1:08]
10	Expectation Waltz, Traditional [1:19]
11	Finlandia, J. Sibelius [1:30]
12	Marche Militaire, Franz Schubert [1:03]
13	Mattinata, R. Leoncavallo [1:51]
14	Sleeping Beauty, P. Tschaikovsky [1:29]
15	Melody in F, A.G. Rubinstein [1:34]
16	Merry Widow Waltz, Traditional [1:12]
17	The Ash Grove, Traditional [0:37]
18	'0 Sole Mio, Traditional [2:10]
19	"Piano Concerto" (Main Theme), S. Rachmaninoff [1:54]
20	The Skater's Waltz, E. Waldtcufel [1:41]
21	Thunder and Blazes, Traditional [1:00]
22	Allegretto (Symphony No.3), J. Brahms [1:01]
23	Menuet No.2, J.S. Bach [1:35]
24	Hungarian Dance No.4, J. Brahms [1:45]
25	Greensleeves. Traditional [1:44]
26	Farewell Song (Now Is The Hour), Maori Melody [2:01]
27	Opening Theme of Symphony No.40, W. Mozart [1:07]
28	Battle Hymn Of The Republic/Battle Cry of Freedom. Traditional [2:26]

1 2 3 4 5 6 7 8 9 0

MEL BAY ®

Visit us on the Web at http://www.melbay.com — E-mail us at email@melbay.com

TABLE OF MUSICAL CONTENTS

Air On The G String . . Suite No. 3 6

All My Trials 52

Allegretto . . . . Symphony No. 3 47

American Trilogy 54

Andante Cantabile . . . . Symphony No. 5 8

Ash Grove, The 35

Ave Maria 10

Barcarolle 9

Battle, The 56

Because 58

Blue Danube Waltz 12

Brahms' Lullaby 13

Carnival of Venice 14

Claire De Lune 16

Dreaming 15

Drigo's Serenade 18

Emperor Waltz 19

Expectation Waltz 20

Finlandia 21

Funeral March 11

Gold and Silver Waltz 22

Greensleeves 59

Gypsy Rondo 23

Happy Farmer, The 24

Hava Nagila 60

Hungarian Dance No. 4 50

Hungarian Rhapsody No. 2 26

Jesu, Joy of Man's Desiring 62

La Cumparsita 65

Largo 68

Maori Farewell Song 69

March From "The Nutcracker Suite" 18

March Slav 25

Marche Militaire 28

Mattinata 30

Meadowlands 23

Melody in F 29

Mendelssohn's Wedding March 32

Menuet No. 2 49

Merry Widow Waltz 33

Mozart No. 40 70

None But The Lonely Heart 34

'O Sole Mio 36

Old Austrian National Anthem 37

On Wings Of Song 38

Piano Concerto No. 2 (Main Theme) 39

Piano Concerto No. 2 (Second Theme) 71

Sarabande 7

Skater's Waltz, The 40

Sleeping Beauty 31

Soldier's March 41

Spiritual Medley 72

Tales From Vienna Woods 42

Thunder and Blazes (Circus) 44

Traumerei . . . . Op. 15, No. 7 46

Triumphal March From "Aida" 45

Vienna Life 48

INTRODUCTION

TO THE PLAYER

This book of selected tunes will help you to become a proficient performer on the chromatic harmonica. Some tunes are easily mastered and some will take an extra effort to perform properly. However, this is the way to grow musically. Challenging music will help you reach your goal of being a good performer. But, there is also a place for "instant gratification" ... that is, to be able to play something right away. In this book there are several tunes that can be deciphered quite readily; *Brahms' Lullaby, Carnival of Venice, Maori Farewell Song, Merry Widow Waltz,* and the *Skater's Waltz* are a few examples. The 12- or 16-hole chromatic harmonica may be used with this book. I hope you enjoy this chromatic harmonica music.

Phil Duncan

TABLATURE

Tablature (arrows and numbers) is provided to help you understand the technique in playing these tunes on the chromatic harmonica. Tablature shows when to blow (arrow up) and draw (arrow down), in which hole (1 through 12) and when to use the button (the circled number). The length of the arrow represents duration of sound.

HOLDING THE HARMONICA

Hold the harmonica firmly in the left hand with hole number one to the left. The left-hand fingers should lie along the upper part of the harmonica and the thumb along the lower part. The right hand should be cupped around the back of the harmonica with the right-hand index finger positioned on the slide button. The heel of both hands should remain together. This hand position could be described as the shape of a "sea shell" ... that is, the tips of the fingers are almost pointing in the same direction (to the right).

VIBRATO

If you open and close the right hand, a wavering tone will begin. As the right hand moves back and forth slowly, a vibrato will result. The heel of both hands should remain in contact, while the right hand moves. Some performers use the last three fingers of the left hand, moving them up and down, to create a vibrato. The air or diaphragm vibrato, used by many wind players, can create a beautiful vibrato. Puffing air in or out of the harmonica in a steady manner while playing a sustained tone will create a vibrato.

TONGUE BLOCKING

Tongue blocking is normally used to play chromatic harmonica. This is a technique in which the tongue usually covers the two left adjacent holes so that the air coming down the right inside of the mouth will enter only one hole to the right of the tongue. Lip blocking can also be used – that is, the puckering of the lips to blow or draw into one hole at a time.

THE SLIDE BUTTON

The chromatic harmonica is actually two harmonicas rolled into one, the C harmonica and the C sharp harmonica. Using the slide button you can play either harmonica. The use of this slide button, located on the right side of the chromatic harmonica, will give accurate half-step tones. By pushing in this button, the tone in that hole will change to a tone one-half step higher. This raises or "sharps" the tone. To lower or "flat" a tone you must move to the left one tone then push in the button to get a lower half step or "flat." Changing octaves will occur; that is, middle C could be played in hole 1 or hole 5. This is done so that you don't run out of harmonica while playing a tune.

For a more in-depth study of the chromatic harmonica, *The Complete Chromatic Harmonica Method* book, video and compact disc by Phil Duncan are available from Mel Bay Publications, Inc. For more chromatic harmonica tunes, the *Great Hits for Harmonica* book and cassette are also available from Mel Bay Publications, Inc.

CHROMATIC HARMONICA

The use of the slide button will give accurate half-step tones on the chromatic harmonica. The 12- or 16-hole chromatic harmonica has been notated in this book. A change of octaves becomes necessary for variety and ease of playing. (*All octaves* on the chromatic harmonica *are the same*, except the tones are higher or lower in pitch.)

Same Notational Level

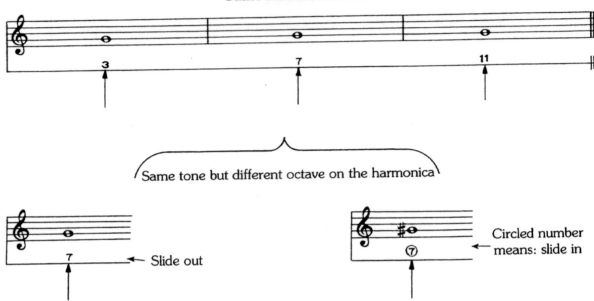

Same tone but different octave on the harmonica

Circled number means: slide in

Slide out

The length of an arrow is for duration of sound:

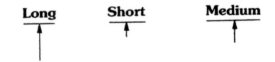

Long   **Short**   **Medium**

The arrow pointing up is *blow.*

The arrow pointing down is *draw.*

16-HOLE CHROMATIC HARMONICA

The 16-hole chromatic harmonica has an additional four holes, or one more octave. This additional octave is attached to the left of the 12-hole harmonica. Therefore, it is the octave below middle C, actual pitch level.

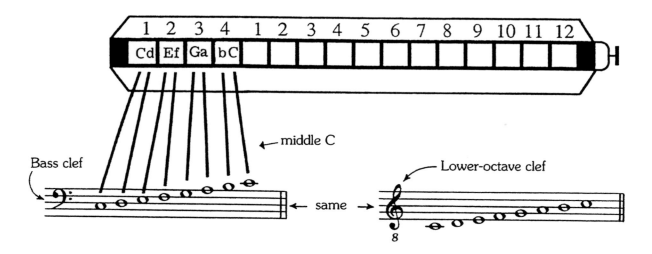

The 16-hole harmonica adds the lower octave so that songs written below middle C can be played on the actual pitch level. It takes less pressure and more air to play the lower octave. The lower octave does not respond as quickly as the upper octaves. It will take practice; but a smooth, easy tone can be achieved.

Lower Octave

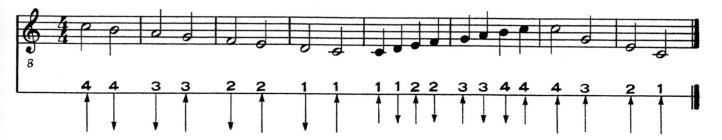

AIR ON THE G STRING
(ORCHESTRA SUITE NO. 3)

J.S. Bach

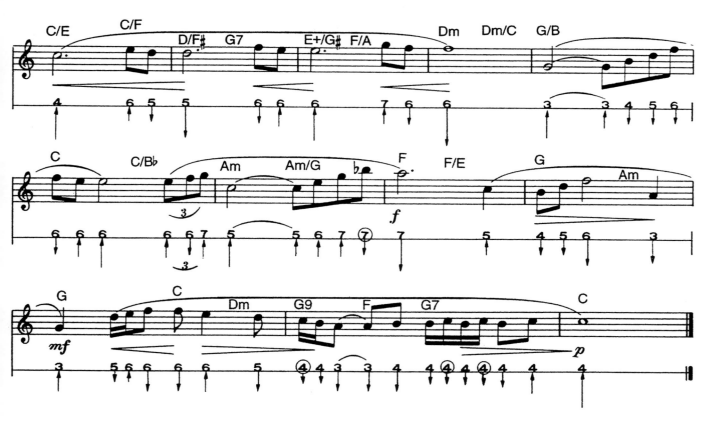

SARABANDE

G.F. Handel

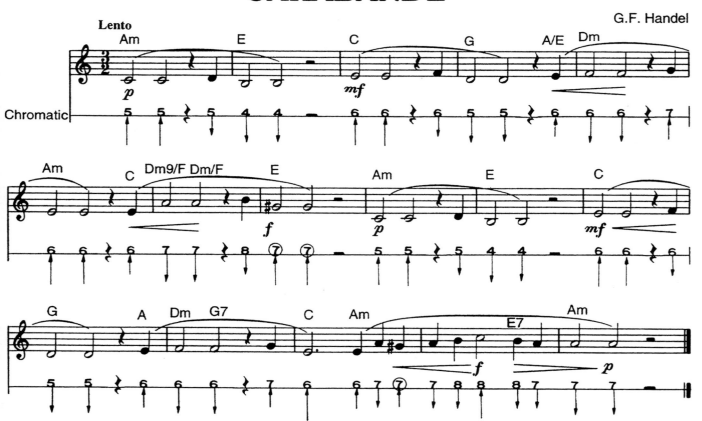

ANDANTE CANTABILE
(SYMPHONY NO. 5)

P. Tschaikovsky

BARCAROLLE

J. Offenbach

AVE MARIA

Franz Schubert

10

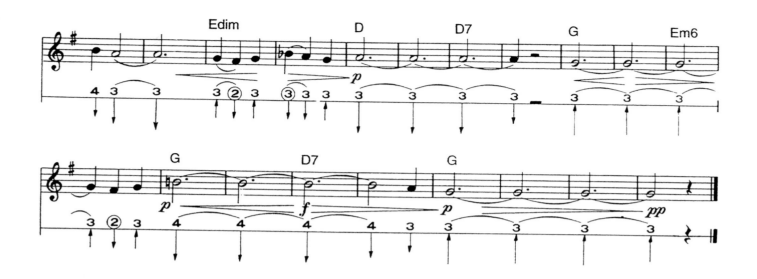

FUNERAL MARCH

Largo

F. Chopin

*BLUE DANUBE WALTZ

J. Strauss

* Can be played an octave lower on the 16-Hole Chromatic.

BRAHMS' LULLABY

J. Brahms

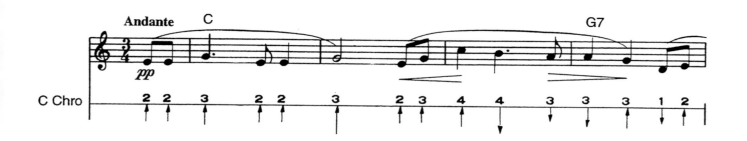

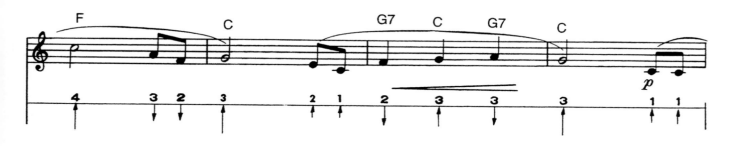

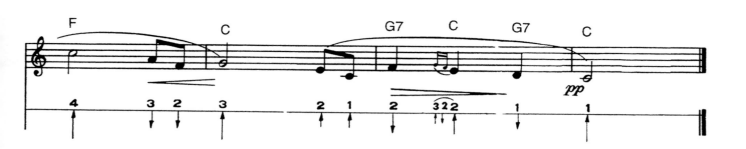

CARNIVAL OF VENICE

J. Benedict

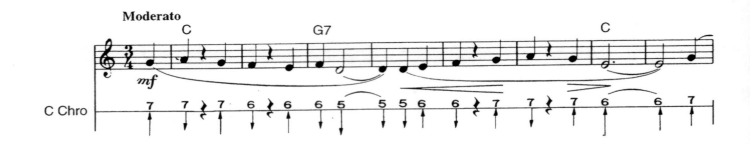

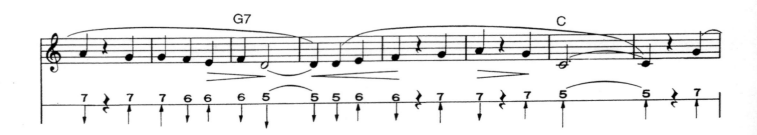

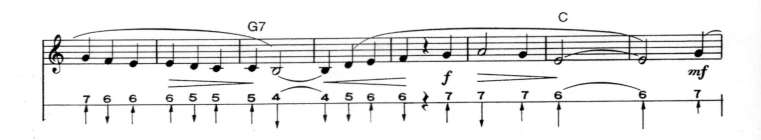

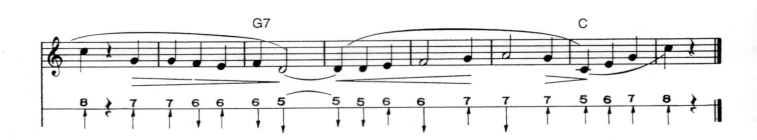

14

DREAMING
(REVERIE)

CLAIRE DE LUNE

C. Debussy

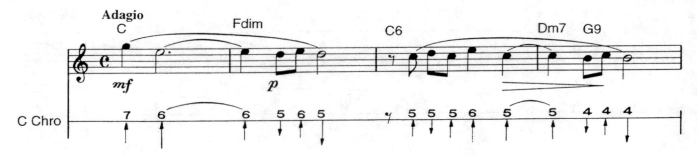

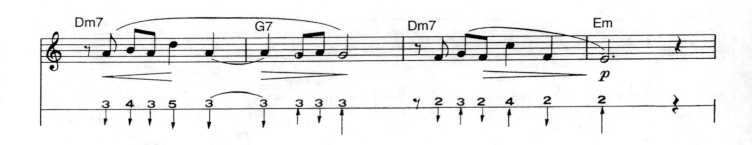

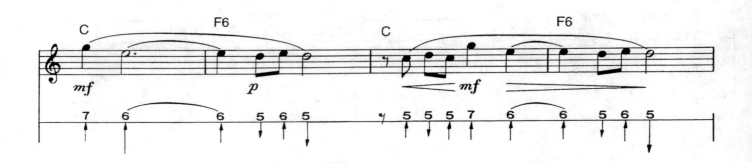

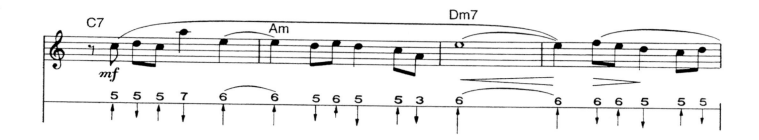

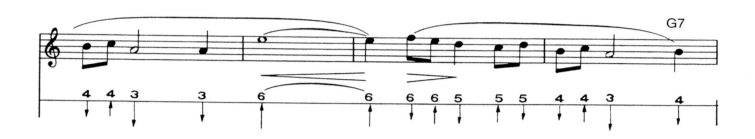

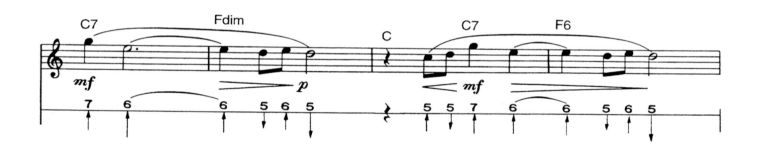

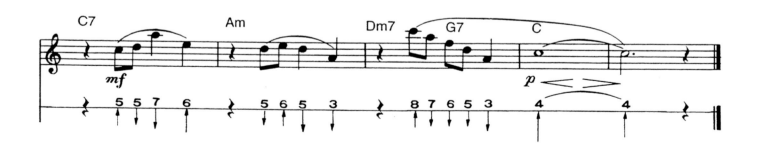

DRIGO'S SERENADE

R. Drigo

MARCH FROM "THE NUTCRACKER SUITE"

P. Tschaikovsky

*EMPEROR WALTZ

J. Strauss

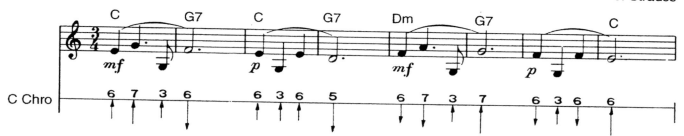

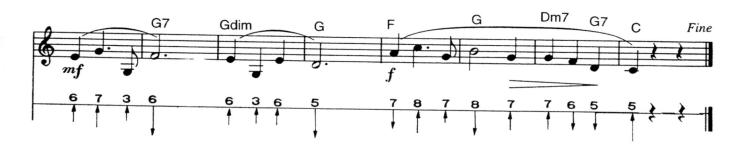

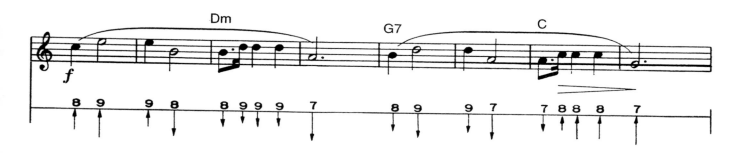

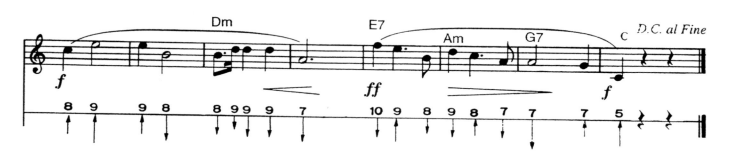

* Can be played one octave lower on the 16-Hole Harmonica

EXPECTATION WALTZ

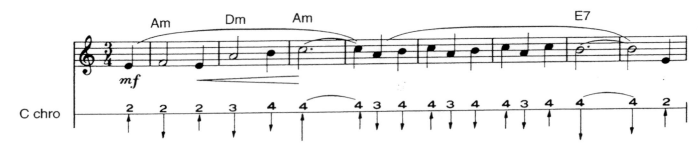

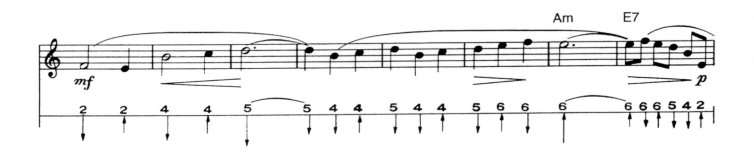

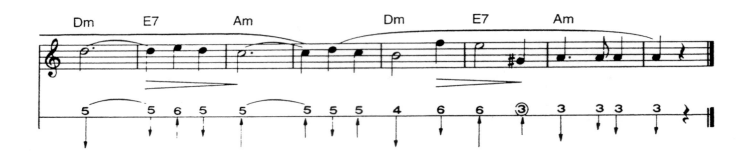

FINLANDIA

J. Sibelius

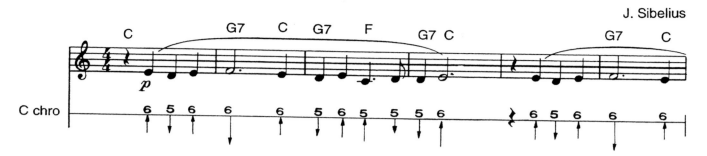

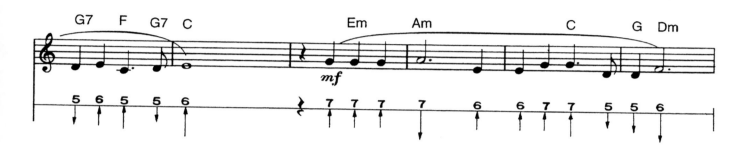

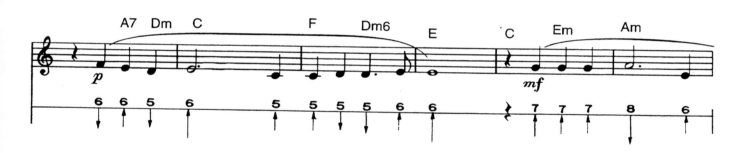

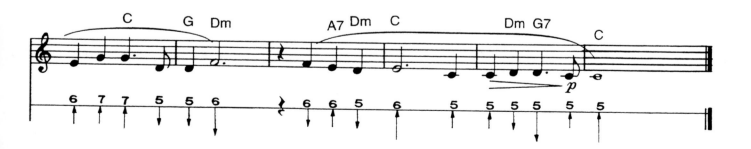

GOLD AND SILVER WALTZ

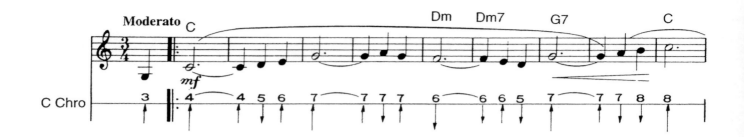

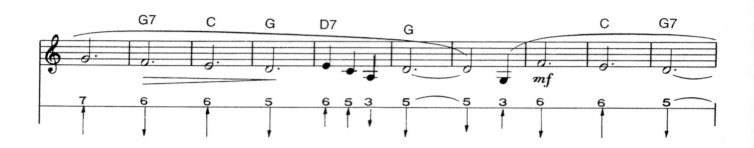

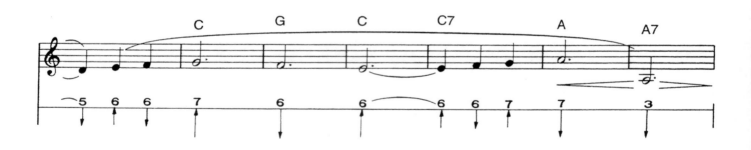

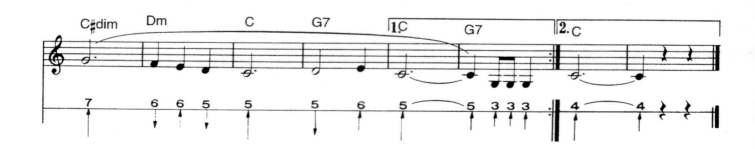

GYPSY RONDO

J. Haydn

MEADOWLANDS

23

THE HAPPY FARMER

R. Schumann

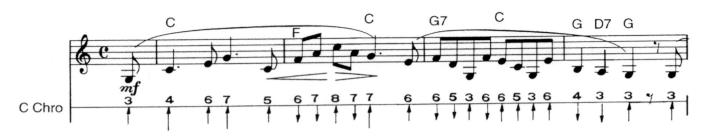

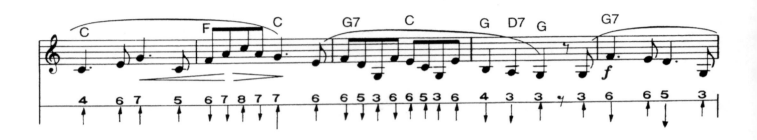

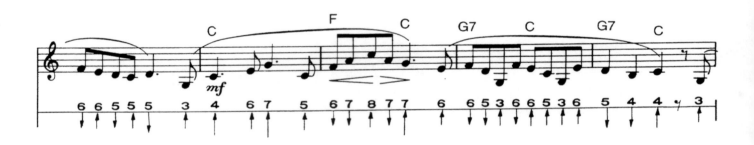

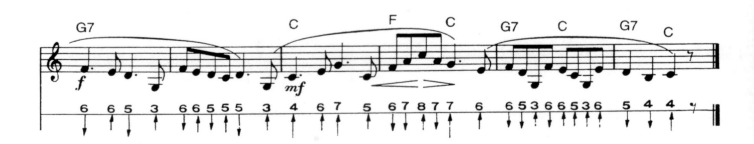

MARCH SLAV

P. Tschaikovsky

HUNGARIAN RHAPSODY
NO. 2

F. Liszt

Allegro

MARCHE MILITAIRE

Franz Schubert

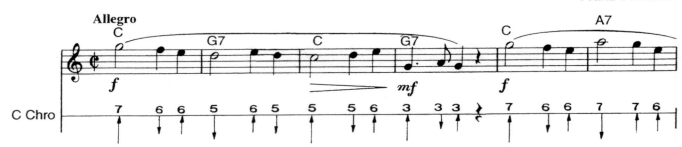

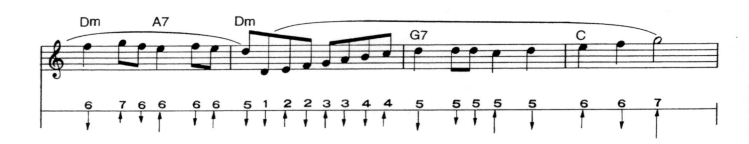

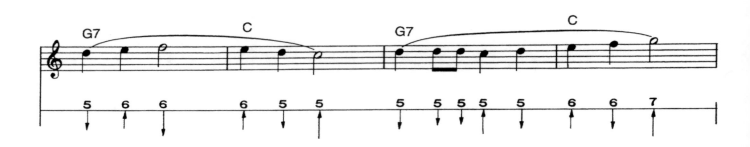

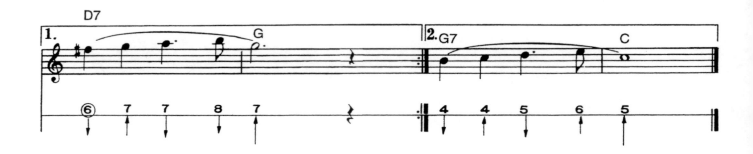

MELODY IN F

A. G. Rubinstein

*MATTINATA

R. Leoncavallo

* Can be played one octave lower on the 16-Hole Harmonica.

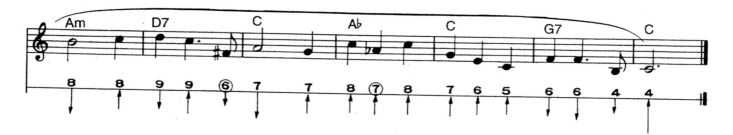

SLEEPING BEAUTY

P. Tschaikovsky

MENDELSSOHN'S WEDDING MARCH

F. Mendelssohn

MERRY WIDOW WALTZ

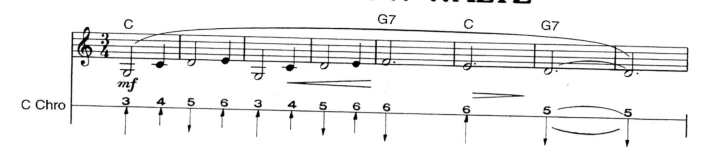

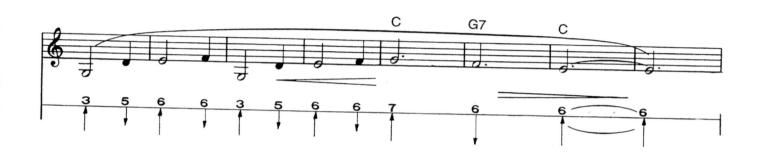

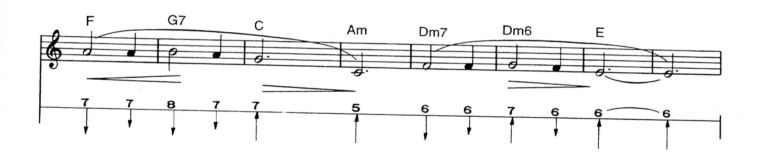

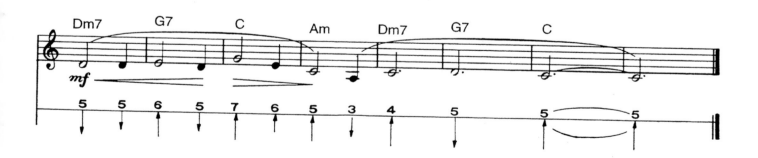

NONE BUT THE LONELY HEART
(OP. 6, NO. 6)

P. Tschaikovsky

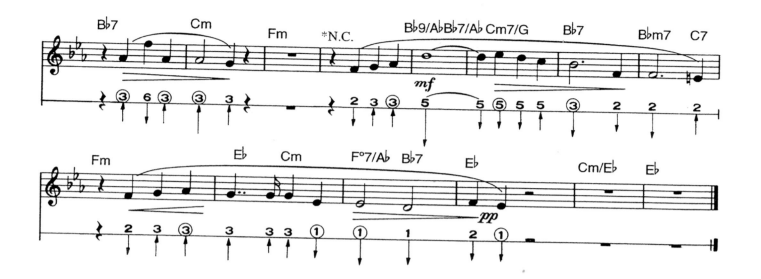

THE ASH GROVE

* N.C., No Chord

'O SOLE MIO

THE OLD AUSTRIAN NATIONAL ANTHEM
(OP. 76, NO. 3)

J. Haydn

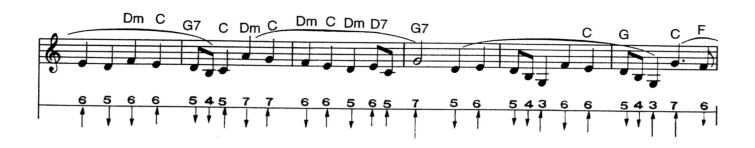

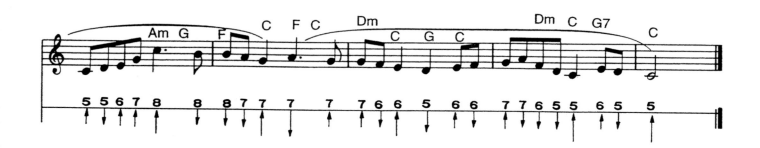

ON WINGS OF SONG

F. Mendelssohn

"PIANO CONCERTO"
(Main Theme)

S. Rachmaninoff

THE SKATER'S WALTZ

E. Waldteufel

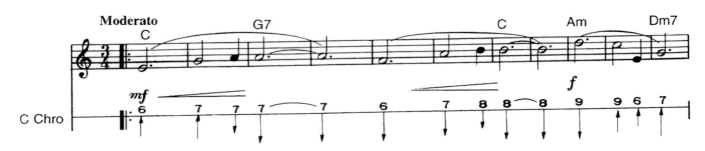

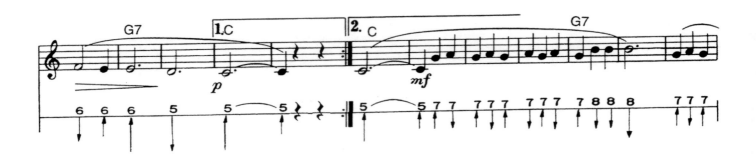

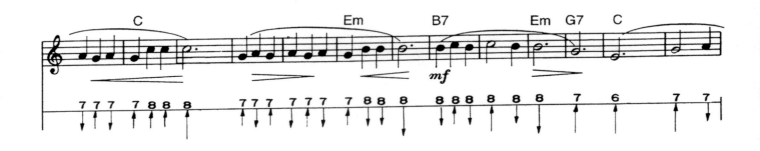

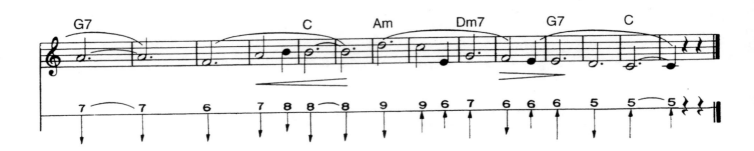

SOLDIER'S MARCH

R. Schumann

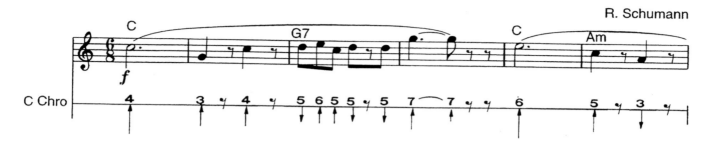

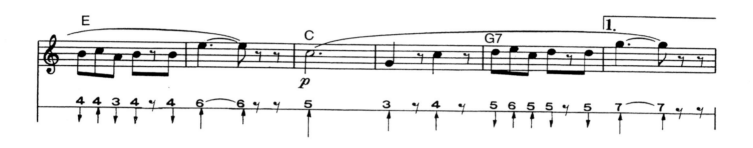

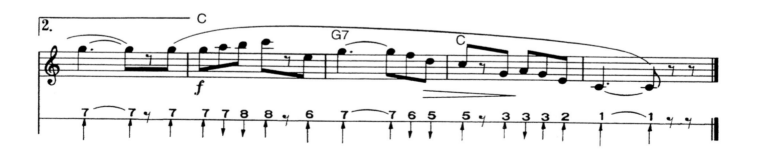

TALES FROM "THE VIENNA WOODS"

J. Strauss

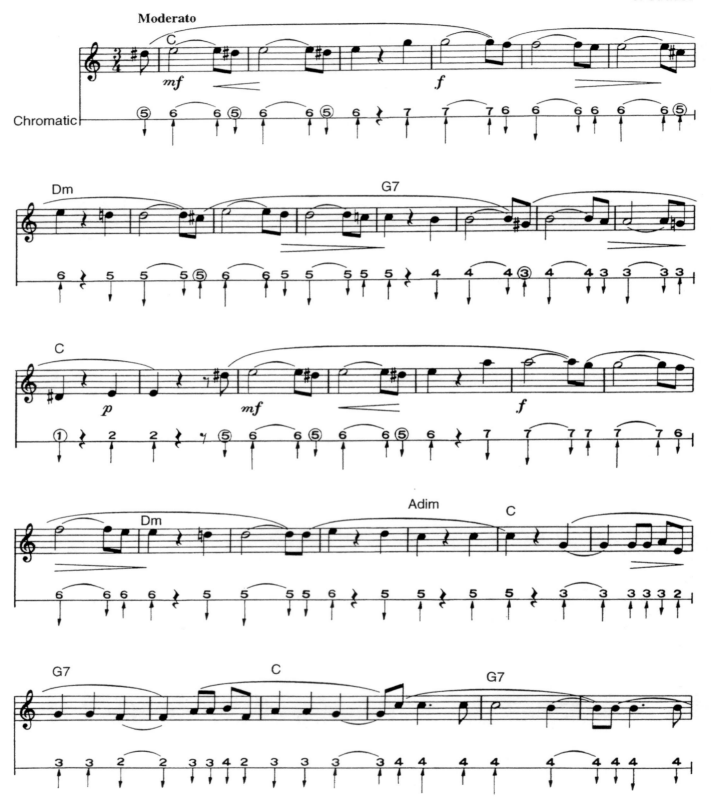

THUNDER AND BLAZES

TRIUMPHAL MARCH FROM "AIDA"

G. Verdi

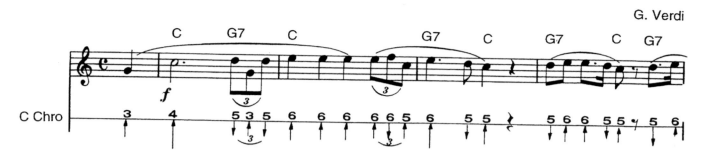

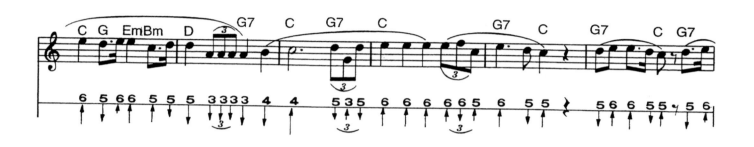

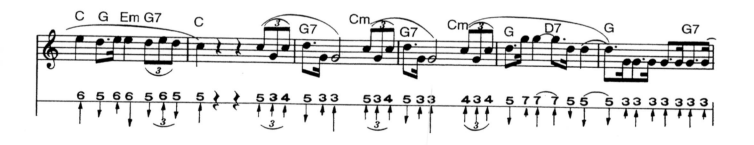

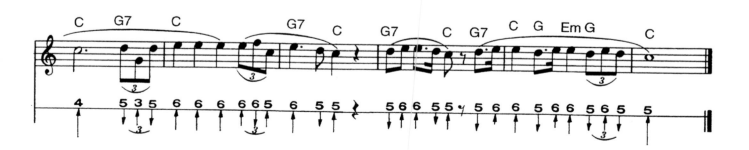

TRAUMEREI
(OP. 15, No. 7)

R. Schumann

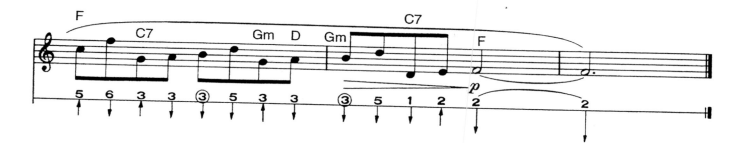

*ALLEGRETTO
(SYMPHONY NO. 3)

J. Brahms

Chromatic

* The 16-hole chromatic can be played one octave lower.

VIENNA LIFE

J. Strauss

MENUET
(NO. 2)

J.S. Bach

HUNGARIAN DANCE
(NO. 4)

J. Brahms

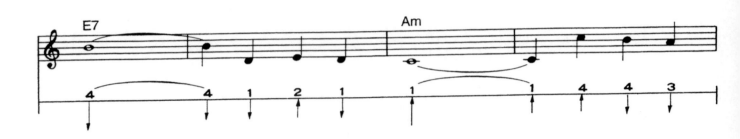

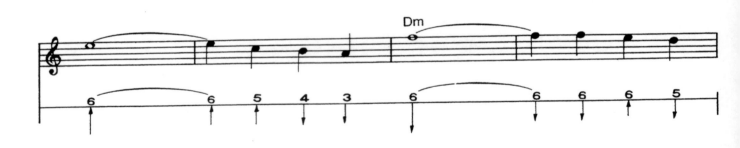

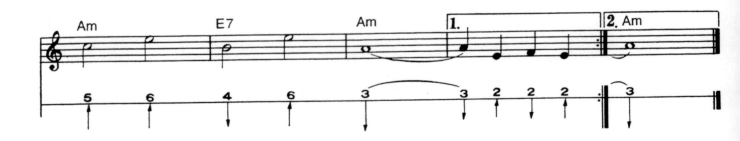

*This page has been
left blank to avoid
awkward page turns*

ALL MY TRIALS

Traditional

AMERICAN TRILOGY

Arr: P. Duncan

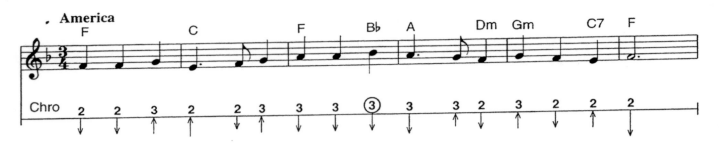

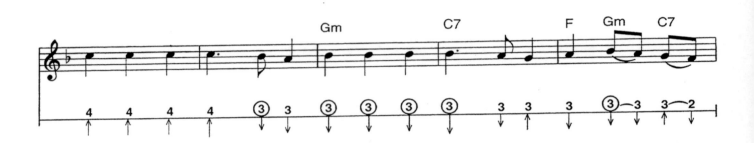

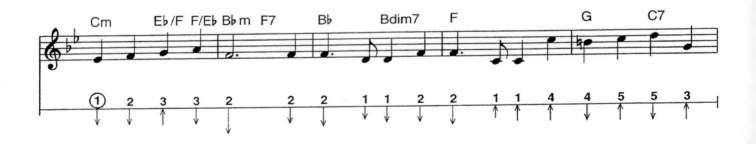

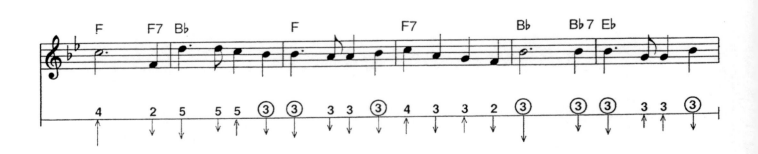

Star Spangled Banner

THE BATTLE

Traditional
Arr. P. Duncan

56

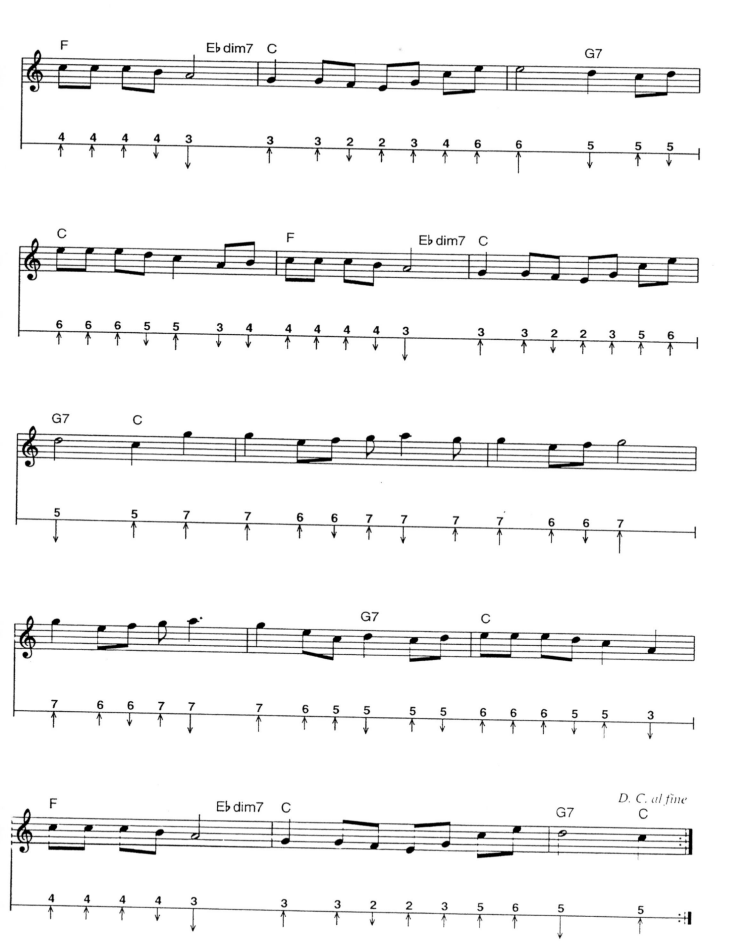

BECAUSE

Guy d' Hardelot

GREENSLEEVES

Traditional

HAVA NAGILA

Jewish Folksong

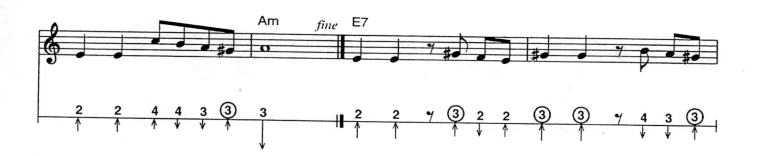

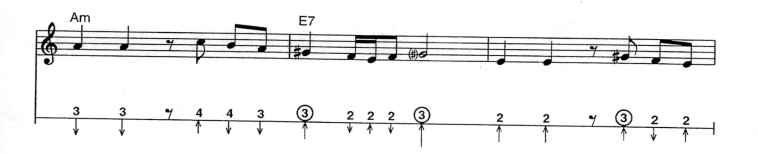

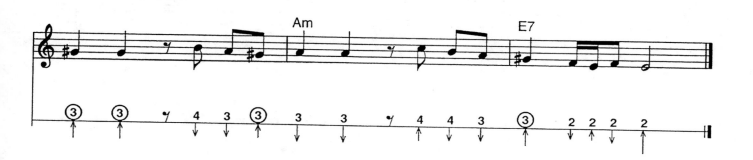

JESU, JOY OF MAN'S DESIRING

J. S. Bach
Cantata No. 147 BWV 147

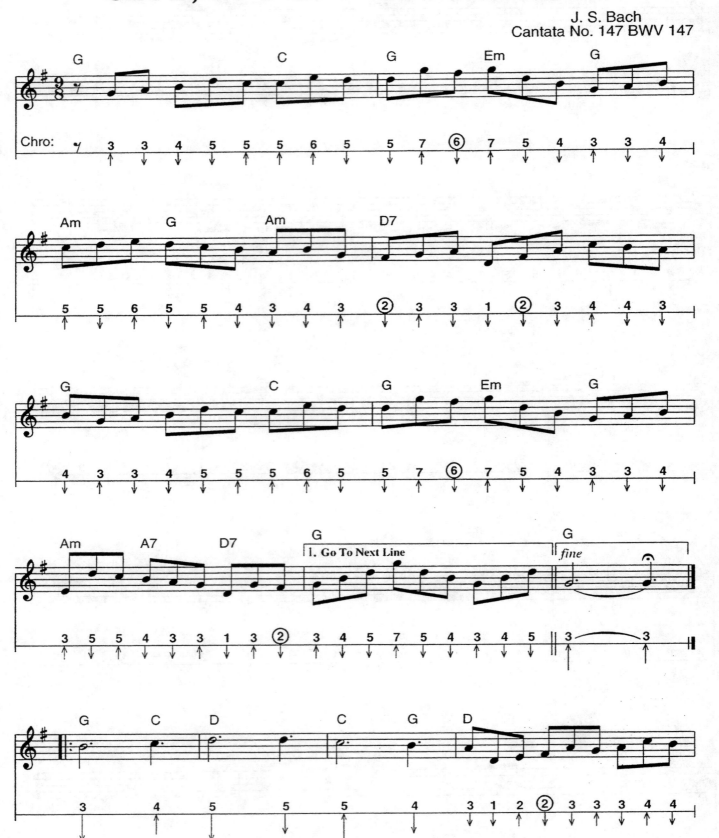

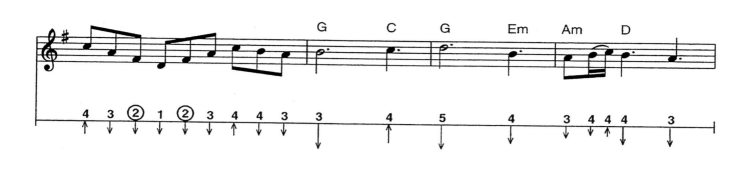

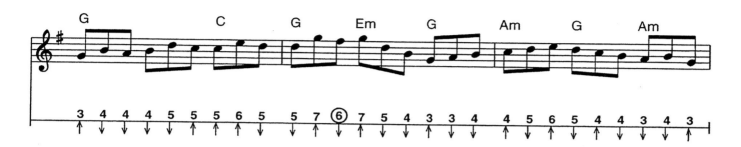

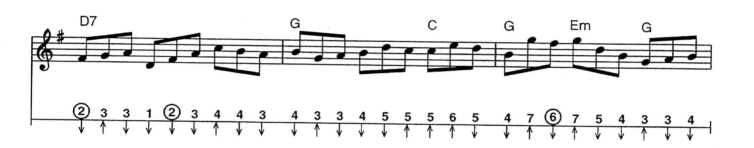

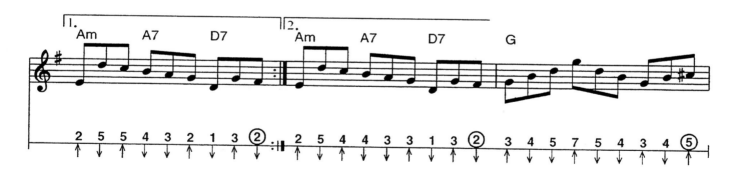

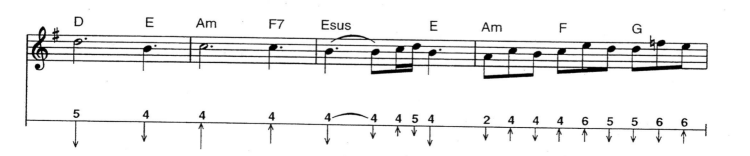

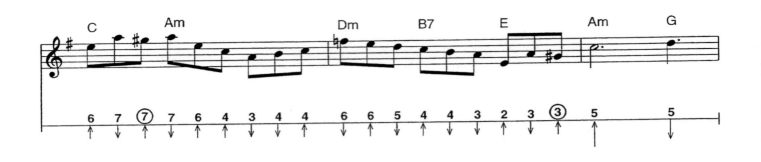

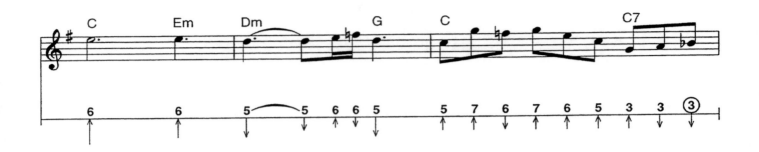

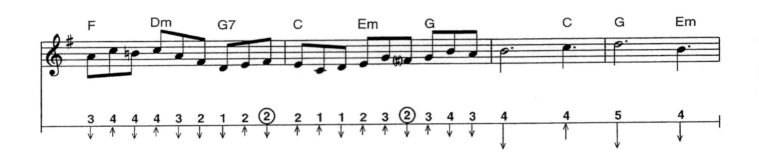

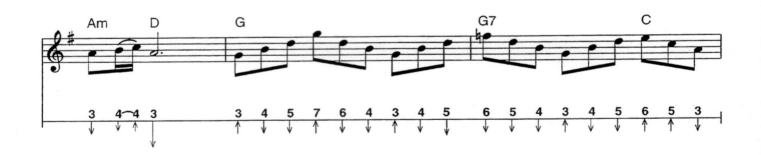

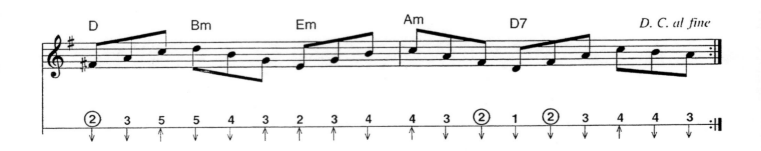

LA CUMPARSITA

Traditional

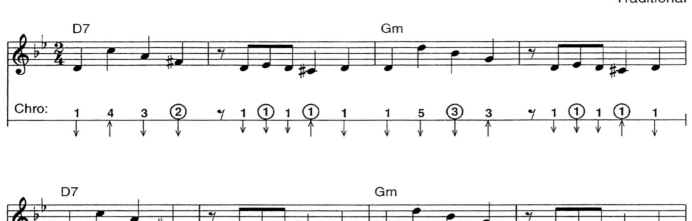

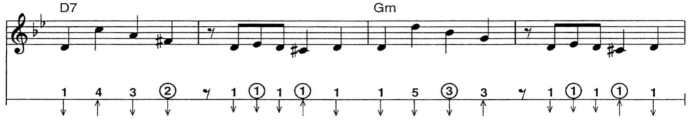

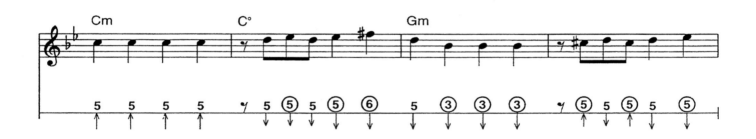

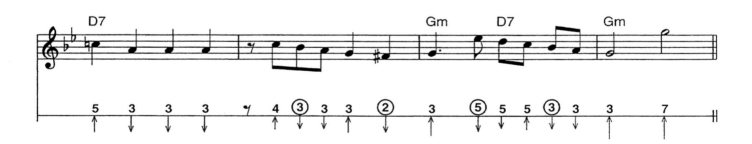

LARGO
(Opera "Xerxes")

G. F. Handel

MAORI FAREWELL SONG

MOZART NO. 40

(K. 550)

Mozart
1778

PIANO CONCERTO NO. 2
(Second Theme)

S. Rockmaninoff

SPIRITUAL MEDLEY

Arr: P. Duncan

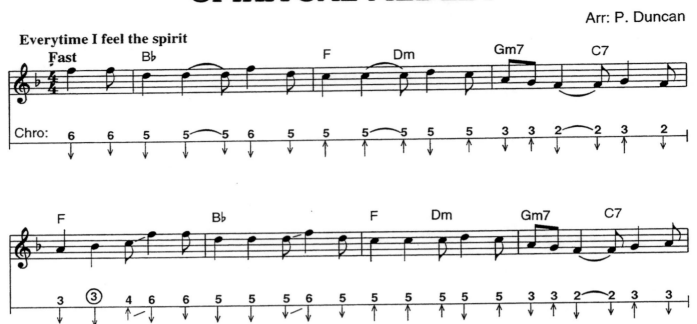

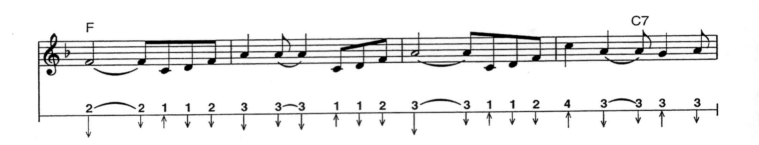

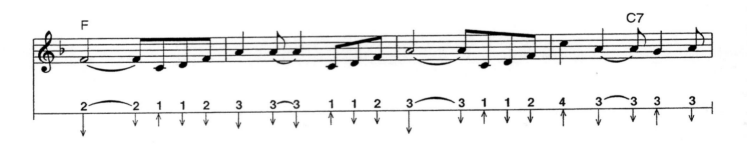

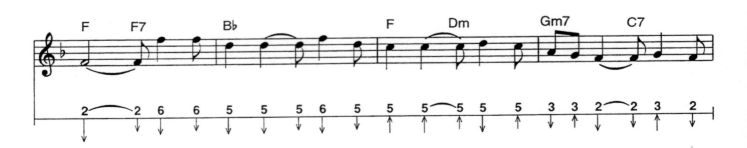

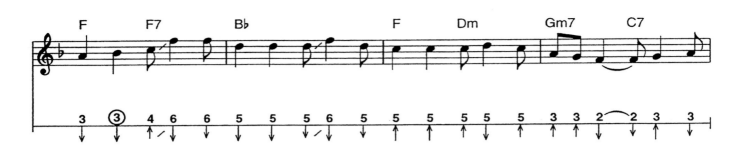

Sometimes I Feel Like a Motherless Child
Slowly

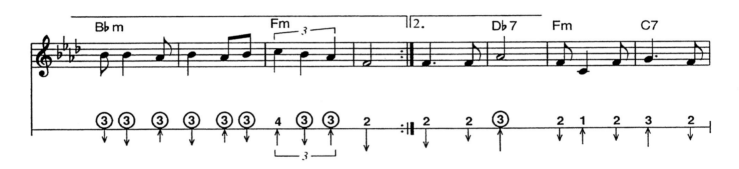

Down By the River Side
Fast

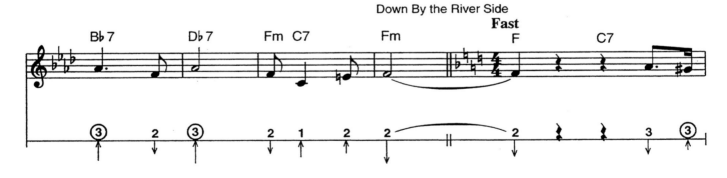

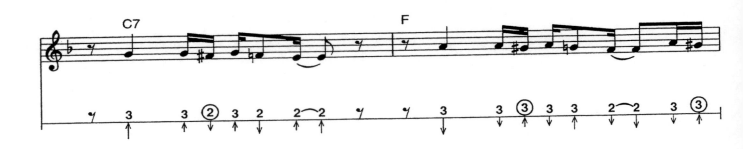

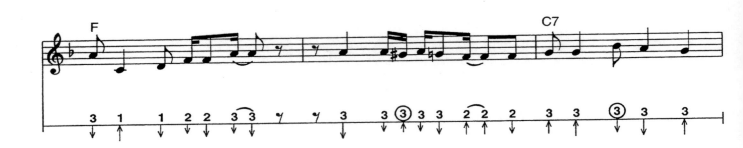

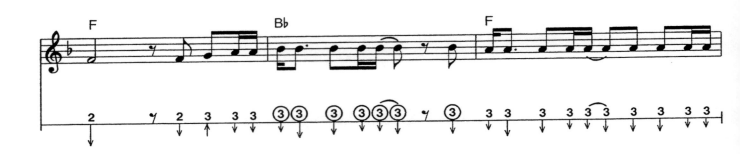

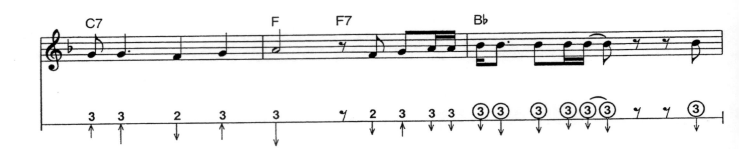

Slow swing

Swing Low, Sweet Chariot

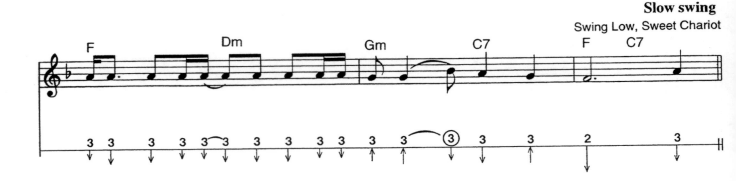